AN HEIRLOOM ADVENTURE!

BY
MARY-MARGARET STRATTON

HEIRLOOM!

Library of Congress Cataloging-in-Publication Data
Stratton, Mary-Margaret (anand)
An Heirloom Adventure! A Raucous Romp and Chicken Chase at the County Fairgrounds.

Summary: "Compelling likeable characters with many laughs throughout. A Summer's-end page-turner in the vein of 'Waiting for Guffman' and 'Best In Show.' Delightful shenanigans happen at the annual harvest festival when the boss of the show goes missing in Mexico on a wild chicken chase!" – Provided by the publisher.

ISBN-13: 978-0-9965835-8-9 (CreateSpace LARGE PRINT)
ISBN-10: 0996583580

1. Literature and Fiction > Contemporary
2. Literature and Fiction > Romantic Comedy
3. Literature and Fiction > Humor and Entertainment

Published by Futura House
2620 South Maryland Parkway #345
Las Vegas, NV 89109
Printed in the United States of America
www.futurahouse.com

Book Photos and Design by MM Stratton (megorama.com) using Century Schoolbook, Copperplate Gothic & Goudy Hand-Tooled

HEIRLOOM!

FETES (A POEM)

The belle of the solar system
spins round in space.

She bows in her blue green floral dress
which compliments her smooth sand skin.

Her airy head is topped with
whispy white wise woman hair.

She is sure of her superiority
among the heavenly bodies,
And she just might lash out
at anyone doubting the fact.

Her moods are seasonable,
but never predictable.
Her womb, a fiery core,
erupts in red hot heat.

But once the matter is resolved,
her deep running life blood water
quenches all who thirst
for romance and love.

~anand sahaja

HEIRLOOM!

HEIRLOOM!

1.

Christine, the festival coordinator, was a sturdy solid sort, who was competent to a fault, and very rarely ruffled, however, the fiddlers really got her riled up this time.

Her hair was neatly braided up into a bun in back, and she sported a long floral pink and green print dress that made her look farm-girl worthy. She was no farm girl though. She was an enterprising gal with a background in botany from some elite West Coast private college. She never studied business, just plants. Her official Botanist Certification had gotten her exactly nowhere, so she was thrilled to be working at the 'Ponticello Stockpile & Seed' store. Somehow, her likeable, proficient, can-do, no nonsense attitude got her the position. She managed a store that sold 'potential' plants and all the accompanying paraphernalia, and that was close enough for her. And true to her character, she stuck with it for the long haul, now an employee with tenure, simply focused on getting things done.

She had a special relationship with George, the Master of Seed, the purveyor of the Stockpile store on the West Coast, and also the owner of the Crimson Creek Seed Company, a non-GMO, heirloom, Organic, Fair Trade, and all around green-living, planet-friendly endeavor in Eastern Texas. Seven years ago, he came up with a concept to throw an annual party for friends of the Stockpile store, and it quickly mushroomed into the International Heirloom Faire, the I.H.F., for short, at the local county fairgrounds. Christine was in charge of making these visions a reality, too.

George was prone to fantasy and had expectations that all of his fanciful dreams could come true. And somehow, it did all came to pass. It did not hurt that the crew of Stockpile fans were also of the sturdy and dependable sort. The people who participated in the show gave countless hours, and the good collective clean sweat of their brows, quite literally, to pull it off.

There were vast fields of summer squash, gourds and vegetables to pick and transport; many individual squash were ten to twenty pounds or more a piece. There were hay bales to stack, stages to construct for the live bluegrass bands, and educational displays to assemble. There was a huge annual display of autumnal vegetables always stacked up in a giant pyramid in the Main Exhibit Hall. And there were all the other usual Faire fixin's that needed to be set up each year at the end of the usually brutally hot central California summer. All this was done by a host of eager zealous volunteers and underpaid staff that did it for the love of seed and show.

The two fuming fiddlers, however, were the last straw for Christine. It was only the first day of the event, and already the foolishness started. All the planning in the world would never prepare her for the follies of free spirits. They came raging into the office at the fairgrounds with a grudge to offer, and demanding justice be served. There wasn't even a cordial, "Hello!" or "How d'ya do?" or "Good morning to you."

Apparently, the winner of the morning fiddling contest has used some questionable techniques to win and the judges were either not privy to the information or turned a blind eye to the atrocity. The winner had used a non-regulation fiddle. What that meant,

HEIRLOOM!

Christine could not fathom. But they claimed it so and wanted it looked into. They were also quite upset that the winner chose a song that the judges knew, making them more amenable to like that player more than the rest. The judges had apparently displayed a startled look when a clever minor chord was played where a major was expected.

Christine frowned, though she smiled inside, "Imagine playing a song that people might know!"

It would be so much better if she could just turn the matter over to George. He had an agreeable, amiable way of making folks feel heard and appreciated. But George was nowhere on site. In fact, no one had heard from George in three days.

George had left the company office Friday morning, literally days before the Faire opening date, in search of some rare heritage breed of chickens that had been purportedly been discovered in northern Mexico. He went off on his wild chicken chase with a crudely drawn map, some rumors, his assistant, Danielle, and a plan to find a local guide to take them into the jungle to find some hidden cave where the rare breed nested. Needless to say, his staff (and wife) were none too pleased to see him fly the coop, so to speak, less than a week before the big occasion. But he promised everyone it would only be a three day adventure and that he would be back in time to cut the ribbon on Tuesday morning. He knew that Christine had it handled, and this was not their first year at the rodeo - so to speak. So the last anyone had heard from him was a broken up voicemail left on Saturday that he to take off in a crop-duster by-plane on Monday morning.

So the fiddlers stood there demanding her attention. She sighed and promised them, "We will certainly have someone look into the matter." And they slowly shuffled out of the room, muttering about fiddle fraud... fiddle fraud...

HEIRLOOM!

Every year, since the beginning, there was always a fiddler contest controversy, a giant pumpkin controversy, a sheep shearing controversy, a honey controversy, and a host of vendor issues to handle. Usually George was there to smooth over ruffled feathers, but right now he was chasing after other feathers.

George Crimson was a mystical creature. Like Christine, he also had a can-do attitude. It's why they rarely clashed and the company ran so well. He started his seed saving company at the tender age of seventeen as a result of a senior year high school project. He quickly found himself surprisingly successful. As more and more farmers and homesteaders were looking for good clean seed, and especially unusual varieties made readily accessible, he had produced a niche market. He embraced his stroke of luck intrinsically, and internally felt it was a sign from God that he was destined to be great - not in an egotistical way, but in a pragmatic manner.

HEIRLOOM!

So he lived his life as such. He married his high school sweetheart and they produced three golden haired girls who lived a fairly normal family life spending half their time on a small farm in Texas, and long hot summers in Central California, near the Stockpile store. No matter what state they were in, George went off to work each and every morning in his blue checkered shirt, dapper pink bowtie, and sensible slightly-worn denim overalls.

The office in Texas was a large two story distribution warehouse which loosely resembled a "Raiders of the Lost Ark" movie final scene with endless rows of labeled boxes and crates. A basement was filled with even more boxes of seeds, still valuable and viable, but expired from years past and non-sellable. These all got regularly donated all over the planet to school gardens and seed banks. George became not just dedicated to seeds, but to the complete homestead experience.

HEIRLOOM!

The Stockpile store in CA was set up in a historic barn where an old army surplus supply used to exist. Some of the old surplus inventory became part of the 'stockpile.' Its accompanying catalog provided everything one might need for an off-the-grid lifestyle. George's company and mission attracted the devout Amish, Mennonite, Seventh Day Adventist, and Later Day Saints (aka Mormon) communities, hell bent on escaping hell. It also attracted the ecology-minded permaculture devotees, extreme survivalists, homesteaders, as well as the esoteric followers of Viktor Schauberger, Rudolf Steiner, et al. The Faire itself, attracted all of those folks and more, as well as, every other person growing sprawling tomatoes in a back yard patch or a sprig of parsley on the kitchen windowsill. Like everything George touched, the Faire became wildly successful. Somehow it all seemed to work, and the soundtrack of bluegrass, strumming, picking and yodeling provided the soundtrack.

So Christine was left to fend off the fiddling folks in a pleasant manner. Her own Mennonite upbringing taught her to be charitable to all, including pesky persnickety fiddler players. Her faith kept her serene on the outside. But deep down, she felt quite upset to be left alone handling the aggravation solo. And the other part of her was concerned that some real harm may have come to their fearless leader. She broke open and sucked on a skinny plastic tube of organic honey to the end using her fingernails to squeeze out every last drop. She picked up a second tube and started in on it, put her mind off the worry, and went back to business.

HEIRLOOM!

2.

On the prior Friday morning, George did a quick perusal of his social stream before work. He blinked. Was it real or Photoshop? George had to know. A friend of a friend from Panama posted a picture of the most beautiful heritage rooster he had ever seen. He whistled a long slow whistle at his phone and spread his fingers to get a closer look. "That's amazing..." in a southern drawl.

The comb and matching tail feathers were on fire. The undercarriage was a brilliant blue, and the top feathers were a mélange of canary yellow and navel orange. Never had he seen such an unusual combination of plumage. A more magnificent species he had not encountered.

The post said the hens supposedly produced the tastiest chocolate colored shell eggs with brilliant orange yolks. It went on to describe the roosters as gentle, intelligent and punctual, and living in some off-the-beaten path part of Mexico. This was a neighbor's cock to covet.

He downloaded the photo to his phone, and sent a note to his friend to inquire about this third party friend who had posted the original picture. Unfortunately, the original post was months old and had only recently been shared. The original poster had disappeared mysteriously from social media since that time, or at least hadn't updated their status in a while, and was unreachable for the time being.

HEIRLOOM!

He was in love. And he was in love with
the idea of bringing these birds to market:
a breed never seen before in person by
common Western eyes. How wonderful
would it be if he could get them to the
Faire in time to share this magnificent
breed with his attendees? He ran
downstairs to get with the family
computer to show his wife and little girls
the image that had captured his lustful
fancy. It was almost enough to make his
wife jealous, but she knew better.
George's heart was true and loyal. He
only strayed for a sharply shorn
Shropshire sheep, a Brazilian bonsai
sunflower, or rare chickens such as these
fine myth-worthy specimens.

He hatched a plan. He knew the Faire was
coming up quick, but he had a very
capable person in charge, Christine, plus
the best, hardiest hard working people on
earth: his company crew and volunteers.
He trusted they could pull it off
successfully without him. His people, he
thought; most of his leads and even down

to the menial laborers, were hand selected by himself. He went on gut instinct hiring people, not necessarily with the best experience or pedigree, but he went with the truest hearts and a sincere willingness to learn and to try. His kind of people. His people were also destined to be great.

A three day escapade would put him back at the Faire a day before opening or on opening day, at the very latest. A man never to mince words or time, he immediately used his exotic tropical fruit grower connections to hook him up with a suitable pilot and scout for the job.

Hector was such a pilot. He used to dust crops with pesticides, but after having many family members personally sickened, and tragically losing a wife and son to a mysterious ailment that he could only conclude was linked back to the chemicals he would spray, he gave up the profitable venture. He retired to flying tourists on stunt missions that would terrify the guests, but also thrill them to

HEIRLOOM!

the point where they would
braggadociously tell friends of their death
defying flights over the jungle. On special
request, he would take off over uncharted
areas to unknown areas of lost ancient
ruins. He knew the land like the back of
his hand. Hector could spot a vine covered
pyramid where others only saw endless
greenery. Where others saw random
ditches in the endless dirt, he could
decipher ancient pictograms. Hector came
highly recommended to George. If anyone
could find the chickens, this was the man.
A man of action, George determined they
would meet tomorrow.

HEIRLOOM!

3.

Danielle was a pretty twenty something with a cute figure, but always dressed modestly. She had a schoolgirl crush on her boss, but it went no further. George treated her like a big brother. He never called her by her proper name. It was always, "Dan." And that was okay with her. She loved his wife and his children as family. She only wished she could find herself such a man to love for her own. In the meantime, she practiced being a faithful woman, by being the best personal assistant she could be. In this particular instance it meant that when George asked her to drive with him ten plus hours in the company pickup to Mexico for the weekend, her answer was without delay, yes.

They crossed the border very late on Friday evening and rolled into their destination: a small nondescript town a hundred miles from the border. George had arranged for two adjoining rooms at a respectable looking motel. "Tomorrow we find our man," he said, and turned in for the night.

The morning started lazily; Danielle had already headed to the local dress shop to see if she could find a serape souvenir. George ordered the local cacao drink and found it bitter and spicy the way he liked it. He asked the 'barista' in broken Spanish, "Donde is Hector?"

The attendant motioned his head towards the gas station across the street, and so George headed in that general direction. As he crossed the street, he saw Danielle heading towards him hurriedly. "What's up, Dan?"

"I think I'm being followed."

"Well, join me. We will go to meet our fly boy."

Hector was tinkering under a grey primer painted 1950s Chevy in the single garage bay and slid out when he heard the footsteps on the gravel approaching. He was expecting these last minute visitors, and was curious about the quest. He shook George's hand vigorously and kissed Danielle's hand in a gentlemanly fashion. As he did this, he heard a throat clear and looked up to see a tall, dark, handsome man in a white linen shirt had also approached.

"That's the fellow," Danielle whispered to George as she ducked behind him a bit.

Hector grinned from ear to ear, and said, "I see you have met our local world-renowned Shaman, Tezca."

HEIRLOOM!

Tezca nodded formally to George and bowed deeply to Danielle. "Estas como un tren, señorita!"

Danielle cocked her head. "What did he say?"

"It's an idi... idio... a phrase. It means you are like... a locomotive."

"A what?!?"

"A train. When a train comes through a small town it's a very big deal. It is momentous. It shakes the earth. It's quite a tribute coming from Tez."

"Pleased to meet you, I'm sure," Danielle said shyly to the Shaman, her eyes meeting his.

And as George reached his hand out to him, which was readily received, he asked, "What do you Shaman about?"

"Tez does not speak much English. He speaks the universal language of truth. His name is short for Tezcatlipoca, meaning 'the smoking mirror.' He gets flown all over the world to look at people directly in their eyes. He transmits some sort of ultraviolet light energy through his eyes. Many people receive profound healings from this vision."

Danielle, who was already looking at the Shaman's eyes, started to blush as he returned her gaze.

"Well, I dunno about that, but you sure do have some mighty nice color there in your eyeballs," said George admiring their clear blue-violet color.

The Shaman sensing a compliment said, "Gracias, senior."

George said, "I was wondering, it would be buenos if... could you all join us at the hotel cafe across the street. And we can sit down, leisurely like, and discuss our plans to find those birds."

Hector replied, "Ee-ho, I have to finish up this engine before nightfall. This was a fairly short notice engagement, senior."

HEIRLOOM!

George gave a thumbs up, "That's true. That's amazi..." Hey, how do you say amazing in Español?"

"Asombroso!"

"Okay. That's asombroso!" He sported a big grin having learned a new way to communicate with his south of the border brothers. "We don't get started on our journey until mañana anyways."

Danielle looked at him quizzically. "Don't you think we should get going asap in order to get back to the Faire in time?

"No, today is Saturday. Just because we have left our country does not mean we are entitled to not observe our weekly day of rest."

The Crimson Creek Seed Company followed a strict Seventh Day Adventist Sabbath. No employee was ever expected or even allowed to work on a Saturday. "You work for me, and if you are helping me here, that would be considered work... so today we rest."

HEIRLOOM!

Hector interrupted, "So sorry senior, but mañana is our dia de Dios. Our holy day. We cannot travel that day. There will be no one to gas up the plane. Our air strip is small and will be shut down. In fact, our whole town closes for mass and family time." He looked at George expecting an outrage. He was pleasantly surprised by the antithesis.

"That's asombroso! We will observe your Holy Sabbath, too! We get started on our journey, mañana's mañana!"

Hector had agreed to take on the quest before he had even met George based on the challenging nature of chasing chickens, and upon the recommendation of their mutual rare fruit-growing friends. He had heard that George was on a crusade against chemicals, and that was also alright with him in his book. Now, however, Hector was really hooked. He knew he had a compatriot. A gringo who respected mañana!

HEIRLOOM!

4.

Back on Tuesday - the opening day of the festival, Chief of Security, Charles H. Worth, "Chucky" for short, started the day at a sprint pace. He was chasing a seventy year old suspected 'seed robber' at a brisk walking pace through the Main Exhibit Hall. Chucky was not a "real" security officer, but a worker in the Crimson Creek distribution center on the loading docks. He had a pleasant, soft, friendly face, who had worked up some serious muscles to compensate for his gentle countenance. He was perfect for

HEIRLOOM!

the annual wearing of the badge gig. He
volunteered to get some basic training and
an official certificate in security, and was
off and running, literally.

The old man was walking quickly towards
the exit and Chucky had to catch him and
his booty before he left the fairgrounds.
Apparently, the old guy had absconded
with a very large portion of the rare seed
display. His tottering, tubby, white-haired
wife created a diversion asking endless
questions about this or that seed, while
the thief deposited as many seeds as he
could into his pant's pockets, jacket,
satchel, and even under his blue and
white striped engineer cap. He would have
gotten away with it, too, except just as the
crime was committed, a group of school
children had entered the hall. Second
grader, Mikey, tugged at his teacher's
sleeve and asked why the old man across
the room was cleaning out the display
before they got there.

HEIRLOOM!

A commotion commenced as someone yelled, "Seed thief!" The wife shrieked and faked a fainting spell - yet another diversion - and the old man moved away from the scene not so fast, hoping not to call too much attention to himself, but it was too late. The attention was already there. Chucky darted from the north end of the room to see what the matter was. He saw little Mikey pointing at the man already fifty feet gone. And Chucky pursued, not initially sure why he was trailing the perp, but he figured it would be best to stop and interrogate the suspect. He blew his whistle and all eyes turned towards him. With right hand on his firearm, he began pursuit, accompanied by the jangling sound of a few dozen keys.

He saw the old man reaching into his pockets and throwing out something from them. He did it again and again. Then a young man ahead to his left, slipped and lost his balance. A middle aged woman on the right hit the floor. He looked down and saw them: seeds... hundreds of them strewn behind the man, leaving a trail of evidence. Knowing he was caught red-handed, the old geezer decided to rid himself of the incriminating loot. He broke into a geriatric run out of the hall and into the light, edging closer to the exit gate. By the time Chucky caught up with him, more seed slip casualties piled up behind them to the left and right. He, himself, almost took a dive into the giant pumpkin display at the south end of the hall. He took a flying leap towards the man; a crowning glory in his life; finally an opportunity to execute his trained response to apprehend a fleeing subject. The once spry old man went down with a crash. Chucky was on it, or rather, on him, making sure he would not reach the exit.

The old man winced as Chucky brought him to his feet. He bawled, "What are you doing to me? Why did you knock me down?"

HEIRLOOM!

To which Chucky replied, "Suspected seed thievery, sir."

The old man retorted faking innocence. "I don't know what you're talking about?"

Chucky frisked him and found the old man had disposed of every last seed on his person. The pockets pulled out were empty, save for a bit of a few tiny unrecognizable seeds, lint and dust. The satchel was also empty.

"But I saw you throwing all the seeds out behind you."

"You saw no such thing young man. I always walk waving my arms," to which he displayed a wild way of walking pretending to mimic the movement.

"You hurt me good. I'll have to see my doctor about this. You'll be hearing from my lawyer."

As he rubbed his neck feigning extra frailty, and tilted his head back. The right edge of his right hand nudged up the back side of his train cap, which miraculously

HEIRLOOM!

had stayed on through the tackle. The hat tipped to the left off his head, and out tumbled a few hundred assorted pumpkin and melon seeds, and a few cloves of garlic. The old man crumbled to the ground and started to moan and shake as Chucky called for backup… and first aid.

HEIRLOOM!

5.

Over in the lecture hall in the afternoon, Squalid Compost owner, Joseph Warden, otherwise known as "Compostable Joe" (or any other combination of manure terms merged in an affectionate way with his name), was giving a talk on the finer negative points of 'humanure.' He was passionate about his subject. He had found a gold mine in packaging certified organic cow dung. He made serious arguments against people poop, and advocated the commodity coming out of the rear end of healthy cattle.

HEIRLOOM!

Joe had been slinging fertilizer for as many years as he could remember. A well-educated man with a business degree from Wharton, he could have peddled almost any good or service. But he hated the restraints of suits and ties and the enclosed office world. He preferred instead to be in cut-offs and Birkenstocks out in the fresh air and sunshine, even if at the end of the day he could not get the stench of the muck out of his nose. He began to relish the scent, not of fresh chewed grass, but of the "fruits" of his labor. And he even developed a high-brow way of describing the various aromas of decomposing droppings. However, today he was full of fresh aphorisms that were especially pungent.

Mothers covered up the ears of their young ones as the profanity ensued. They quickly shuttled the little ones out of the hall shaking their heads and clucking. A few marched straight to the Faire office and aired their grievances to the beleaguered Christine, who had just dealt with an altercation between the giant pumpkin weighing competition participants. The winning pumpkin had an unknown, indeterminate scar of some sort on the bottom and was suspected of being injected with extra weight. A contestant cried out, "There should be a re-inspection," of the winner, except that right after it was weighed in it leaned off the scale and split. The pumpkin owner was adamantly against his pumpkin being harmed any more, saying that the blemish was caused by the scale accident. Christine and the sore loser went to check in with the official Pumpkin Consortium. Being that the giant winning pumpkin was such a sorry sight, the Consortium 'weighed in' on the matter and decided to let the award stand. The sore loser walked away saying, "I'll take my other giant pumpkin to the North Moon Bay competition. I know I'll get a fair shake there!"

As he left, Christine mouthed the words to herself, "My 'other' giant pumpkin???"

HEIRLOOM!

Now her attention was back to the manure at hand. Reports had come back to Christine last year about Joe's language, and she'd had a talk with him about it. She told him, "Leave the foul language for the chicken farmers, Joe!" and she thought herself very clever for the pun. However, it seemed that he had let that talk decay to dust in his brain.

Harold, who managed all of the speakers, and the complete lecture lineup, was supposed to keep an eye on presenters and entertainers to make sure everyone was on time and on topic (especially Joe). He was in charge of anything to do with the audio visual equipment: mics, speakers and projectors. He had a couple of assistants to help him, so with three lecture hall locations and the main stage to manage, apparently he somehow failed to show up at that one particular talk. Christine knew that was probably intentional. Harold hated confrontation, and Joe was a bit of a steamroller. She also knew Harold liked to sample the fermentation tasting stations and elderberry wines in the Vendor Hall after lunch.

After Joe's presentation, she got up spontaneously and thanked the audience for their attendance and for their endurance of his 'colorful' talk. Then she approached Joe. Just as she did, Harold rolled into the room, but when he saw Christine, he made a 180 turn to leave.

"Harold!" Christine waved her index finger at him, suggesting he join the conversation. Harold saddled up between them but remained silent.

"Now Joe, you know you can't use that kind of language. This is a family event. And Harold, you were supposed to be here to keep Joe 'G-rated.'"

Joe apologized up and down about his performance. He explained that the last couple of months had been especially tough for him. His 'factory' had been recently cited for leaking toxic fumes, and dealing with the community open houses had totally burned him out. "They know what we're doing in there. What's the big fuss?"

Losing her usual, unvarying, external cool, Christine snapped back that she didn't care what was going on in his personal life, and that he had an image to maintain. She read him the riot act in no uncertain terms. She told him he was an important representative of the show, (and of all that was possible about recycled bio-solid waste management). He was the voice and he *was the face* of clean compost. "Are we clear?" She pulled two honey tubes out of her pocket, chewed the end off ferociously and sucked down on them as the two gentlemen stared at her in stunned silence. Then she turned around and left.

Harold looked at Joe, winked, finally spoke up, offering him his flask. "You wanna nip, shit face?"

6.

Backtracking to the weekend, Danielle had agreed to have the Shaman show her around the village. And Hector had agreed to head over for a cerveza with George after work to discuss plans. "We take my muy grande plane." George had left a voicemail for Christine on Saturday that due to the double Sabbath, they would not be heading out until Monday, and to expect them back at the very earliest on Tuesday, but most likely on Wednesday.

HEIRLOOM!

At the crack of dawn on Monday morning, they took off in Hector's by-plane. A 'muy grande' plane simply meant four-seater plane instead of the two-seater. It was a perfectly restored and maintained open cockpit 1929 model D-25 with a Wright R-760-8 radial engine of 235 horsepower, built for barnstormers of a long forgotten era, but upgraded with larger fuel tanks for longer flights. It was equipped to carry four passengers in the front cockpit (or three passengers and a bunch of chicken crates), with the pilot holding up the rear. Hector handed them cloth helmets, with professional headsets attached, and goggles.

Being newly enamored of George, Hector wanted to show off his best plane and his best flying, and immediately expertly executed an extraordinary aerobatic roll maneuver. George and Danielle held on for their lives. "Yikes!" George cried as his cell phone slipped out of his upper overall pocket and disappeared into the deep green tangle below.

HEIRLOOM!

After the move Hector shouted up to them, "You okay?"

"Yes. However, I lost my phone! You said, 'tie down your valuables.' You didn't say 'Button your pockets!'"

"We're going where there will be no phone trees."

They spent the rest of the day flying back and forth across miles and miles of emerald forest and barren stretches of dirt, looking for the cave according to George's crude map. They finally had to circle back to the village to refuel. "I think tomorrow we find," said Hector.

"You mean we can't go back out again today?" asked George.

"No, senior, a pilot must rely only on his eyes in this kind of plane. There are no instruments to fly by. It is getting late, and without the daylight, we will not see anything. We could get very lost and that would not do well. Es no bueno."

HEIRLOOM!

When Tuesday morning rolled around, Hector said he had an idea about an ancestral village he had heard tale of that brought extraordinary fruits and legendary eggs to market, but only every quarter season. "They mostly keep to themselves. I have never been up there, but I have heard many tales about them."

"That's asombroso!" George thought about the Faire opening up that morning, and he sent a prayer to wish his people well, and that everyone would be happy and content.

Danielle then piped up, "If it's okay with you, I would like to stay on the ground today. That way, if you find the chickens, there will be more room in the cockpit to bring them back." Secretly she was hoping to spend more time with the Shaman. Something about him when she stared into his eyes gave her a feeling like she was home. And George sensed that his prayer for happiness may have just hit closer to home.

HEIRLOOM!

"Señorita. I think that Tezca will be very pleased to hear this. Jorge! Vamanos!" exclaimed Hector.

They took a turn due East and headed straight to and through a tall set of mountains. It looked like they would crash as they narrowly skimmed through a canyon. Hector's able piloting skills got them through though, and they found themselves soaring over a small fertile valley which had been transformed into patches of well-tended fields. They could see lush rows of maize, and long vines with robust, deep ginger pumpkins.

"Well, I'll be. It's like Shangri La," exclaimed George.

Hector found an untended field of grass and set the plane down gently. The noise of it obviously attracted the curious natives, and they came running to greet them. When George and Hector got out of the plane, Hector spoke to them in Spanish, introducing themselves and their quest. He then said to George, "They speak a very different dialect and it is very tough to understand. But I think we have found your gold!"

The locals were dressed in very brightly dyed clothes. Everything about them was intense and colorful. Their smiles were broad and shiny. Their hair was deep blue-black, and their skin tone was a rich, unblemished burnt sienna. One of the women beamed with pride at the visitors and motioned that they follow her. And it was as simple as that. The mythological birds matched their masters with brilliant colors George had never seen before. The cock's comb was the radiant color of lit up brake lights. The orange back wing feathers were especially long, untrimmed and iridescent in the sunlight.

More words passed between Hector and the woman. She shook her head over and over and kept saying, "No. No. No!"

"It seems that we may be out of luck, amigo Jorge. These birds are not for sale."

HEIRLOOM!

Knowing how far he had come only to be
denied his opportunity, George sat down
on a rock and went deep into thought. He
waited for a vision, but none came. And it
was getting dark; too dark to fly home.
The impending night reflected his mood.

7.

Wednesday morning had been grueling for Chucky. The lead singer of the Fabulous Crimson Cousins (the name being a coincidence, as they had no familial relation to the Crimson Creek Seed Company) was as beautiful and as talented as they come. She had a voice like Frances Ethel 'Baby' Gumm, that was big and broad, well beyond her earthly years. The family bluegrass band started to perform at the event when she was just eight years old. Cute and perky then, and now she was blossoming into a rare beauty beyond measure. The attendees took notice of this lovely young lass. People sat up and paid more attention to the music this year. One young man fan in particular especially took notice and began stalking the girl after she left the stage. The Crimson Cousin girl's mother reported this to Chucky who started to stalk the stalker. While the band was on the bandstand, Chucky met up with the shifty guy behind the Grange booth off to the right of the stage. He had stationed himself there to keep tabs on the object of his desire while she was performing. Chucky questioned the creep. He was late twenty-something with a green t-shirt that said, "Keep the Culture in Agriculture." His hair was a little too long to be called a mullet; just a bad nineteen eighties stringy hair with a lean lanky look. His goatee was sparse and dirty blonde. His face was weathered. He had been out in the sun too much, or drank too much beer in his short lifetime, or a lot of both. He watched the girl, dreaming of his own lost youth, thinking that if he could just marry her, his life might turn out all right after all. He could not take his eyes off her, even as Chucky approached and spoke to him.

Chucky found his name to be Garth. He said he was just enjoying the music, but Chucky informed him there had been a complaint against him, and that he would have to leave the fairgrounds and not return. His entrance fee would be happily refunded. The sparkle in Garth's eyes grew dark as he turned to face Chucky.

"I can't leave her. She's expecting to see me after this set."

"That's just it. She doesn't want to see you. You have to leave."

Chucky gently took him by the arm and began to escort Garth to the rear gate as he protested. "Nah... Nah... Please man. You gotta let me see her finish. I gotta see her one more time. She's my angel."

HEIRLOOM!

The pleading and protesting continued as Chucky nudged him through the exit turnstile.

"You don't come back here ever again. Got it?"

"Okay," as Garth sheepishly walked towards the parking lot.

Chucky walked back over the bandstand, sat down and grabbed a pulled BBQ pork on a multigrain roll, and enjoyed the end of the set while keeping an eye on the crowd. As the band headed to their CD sales table, he watched the fans come up and examine the music and t-shirts. Then out of the corner of his eye in the line to buy, he saw a familiar face he could not place. Then it clicked. He recognized Garth in a crisp long sleeve button down denim shirt sporting a red baseball cap. The Crimson Cousin girl shrieked as Chucky strong-armed the man leading him back through the exit again.

HEIRLOOM!

"Don't you ever try that again, man. We'll be looking out for you."

After briefing the ticket takers at the entrance booths to keep an eye out, Chucky proceeded to head back to the Faire office for a few minutes of down time with Christine. Christine offered him a honey tube and he readily accepted. Not ten minutes later, the Crimson Cousins girl came in teary eyed and trembling, followed by her husky stage mother, sobbing, "He's back. He looks all freaky and different, but I know it's him. I just know it."

"If you can't take him Chucky, I will." And the Crimson Cousin matron looked like she could almost do it. She was a strapping woman of five foot five. And Chucky wondered how that delicate blooming flower of life could have come from such a burly built woman.

Chucky got out of his chair. Christine looked at them all inquisitively.

HEIRLOOM!

"We got a singer stalker." Christine nodded, grateful that this was his problem, and not hers. Chucky said to the Crimson Cousin girl, "You sit down here with Christine and she'll look after you." He proceeded to walk out the back door to the office and circled around to the front of the building. He scanned the crowd looking for the green t-shirt or the blue long sleeved short. No luck. He looked for unusual behavior or body language, just like he learned in his security training videos. Nothing. Then, on a hunch he looked closer at a body in a wife beater and a set of overalls hunched over a vendor table just around the corner from the Faire office. He knew those sloped shoulders well by now. But the hair was different. It was sheered short, military style. He walked up to the personage, and there he was, fully clean shaven, but with the same faraway crazed look in his eyes.

"What is wrong with you, man? Don't you know the lady doesn't like you? You have been ordered out of here two times now. This is your third strike brother."

Garth looked at him calmly replying, "I changed everything for her. I can be the man of her dreams."

"More like her nightmares. Com'on buddy, let's go," and Chucky once again grabbed him roughly by the arm and escorted him off premise. "Don't you ever, ever come back here again, or we'll have you arrested for trespassing."

The next hour went by uneventfully. Finally, the Crimson Cousins came back for an afternoon set and the crowds were happy to sit it out in the shade enjoying the after-luncheon music. Chucky hung around for moral support for the once shaken young lady. A lively banjo tune started up and the Crimson Cousins egged the crowd to clap along and dance on the lawn if they felt inclined. A few kids were already moving to the music, as children do, down in front. A tall brunette lady in a long cowgirl dress and brown boots was blowing soap bubbles towards the children, much to their delight. When the band suggested dancing, she stood up in front of the band swaying and clapping to the tune.

Moments later, the Crimson Cousin girl's voice cracked. She kept singing, but something was off, and the band all had strange looks on their faces. A sour note came from the mandolin, then the banjo. The lady started blowing kisses to the singer and everything in Chucky's vision slowed down to crawl as the realization that this was no lady dancing.

He rushed the stage and tackled Garth in front of the crowd and the band's tune came to a screeching halt. Garth screamed in a high pitched voice, "Let me go. Let me go. My angel! My angel!" He screamed, squirmed, cried and flailed. His wig dislodged from his head, and Chucky could barely hold him down as he shouted out to the crowd, "Somebody please call the cops!"

HEIRLOOM!

A lady in the crowd said, "Wait. Aren't you the cops?"

"No ma'am. I'm the security."

8.

Ponticello Paul (Smith) was a champion piano player of the American Standard songbook, combined with a little Lennon and McCartney. Every year he got hired to entertain the passers-by with his red, white and blue festooned portable honky-tonk piano on wheels. And every year the vendors vied for the spaces furthest away from his worn-out tunes. It was not so much the quality of his playing. He was a snappy and accomplished player with fast fingering. It was just that hearing "God Bless America" every other hour, and "Ob

HEIRLOOM!

La Di Ob La Da" on the other hour, and a repetitive repertoire in between, was too much to handle for three days straight.

And every year, there were issues with vendors. One of the hot sauce vendors had to be shut down, because their 'Gates of Hell' hot sauce rated so high on the Scoville scale, they sent several sampling attendees to the emergency room. Although the chocolate vendors had no official competition, they were always snooty about whose chocolate was superior, and they claimed that the fudge people should not be allowed in the Vendor Hall, because someone said they used standard genetically modified C&H sugar in their recipe, not organic sugar.

The various plant and seed vendors were amicable towards one another, as this was the one show where they were all assured decent amount of sales. Unlike the typical flea market situation where they were lucky to give away a rare fig cutting, or package of bitter melon seeds, here their audience was hungry and enthusiastic about their wares. Each compared their offerings with the others, often trading seeds and slips like baseball cards.

While walking past the food vendors, Christine overheard some left-wing environmental activists complaining about how there were no compost bins available for all of the food scrap leftovers and such. She twisted around and shot back at them, "Take your scraps to Compost Joe!" Thinking to herself, "That would be reward for yesterday. Let him deal with the rabble."

It dawned on Christine that there still had been no word now from George for four days. She held onto the idea that it was just a matter of inadequate cell phone service wherever they were, and sold that story to anyone who inquired. It had been a fairly choppy connection when he called on Saturday. That was it. She would believe that story and have faith. In the meantime, vendor rounds were on tap.

HEIRLOOM!

The honey vendors were the most sensitive of all. They were overall a quiet and calm lot with nerves of steel, considering their occupations. Every year there was a tasting test done by a shady looking character who was alleged to be a honey expert, but somehow no one ever saw his credentials other than a full color coffee table book, entitled, <u>Being Kind to Bees</u>. He went into a private room for an hour with his refractometer and came out with a blue ribbon for the same beekeeper for the last three years running. Another beekeeper began to grumble that last year he was turned away from the competition for not having the correct jar requirement, while this year, all different sizes of jars were accepted.

To overcome future hullabaloo, Christine initiated a secondary public 'People's Choice' tasting award this year, in addition to the back room judging. She thought it might provide a more level playing field. However, this ended up with accusations of ballot stuffing. To make

HEIRLOOM!

matters worse, some unknown and disgruntled beekeeper had poured an entire jar of honey over Paul's keyboard which stopped his playing for several hours while volunteers attempted to clean it up. There were no complaints about this from anyone, except Ponticello Paul, who became known as Sticky Fingers Smitty from thence forward.

Christine loved the honey vendors nonetheless. She had a huge collection of bee collectibles: mugs, teapots, cookie jars and more. Antique honey dippers were her favorite find at swap meets and estate sales.

Every year at the Faire, the honey vendors always supplied her with a bucket of seemingly unlimited honey sticks that got her through the event. She related to the busy little worker bees. She thought, "Like me, they're getting their thankless botanical jobs done in complete harmony with nature. And George is my queen bee." She couldn't help it. She imagined

HEIRLOOM!

him with a seed studded crown and
scepter and an ermine yellow and black
striped mantle, and laughed. "Strike that.
I will need to work on a better analogy."

HEIRLOOM!

9.

When George and Hector realized they would not make it back to their base village Tuesday night, they decided to make the best of the situation. The colorful citizens of "Shangri La" took them in and offered them their hearts and homes. They were a jovial people, amiable and open. After a hearty meal of the best huevos and queso blanco he had ever eaten, George told them about his personal mission to save seeds and to fighting against genetically modified organisms. This proved very difficult for Hector to translate, because in this little valley there was no 'evil agriculture empire' to wrestle with, and everything they had was of heirloom quality. The industrialized world had not affected them other than to provide them with better tools for planting and harvesting. They were such a little and far off land, they had not been affected by the greedy ways of the Modern world, as of yet.

George had brought muchos pesos, which the villagers had promptly declined to exchange for the chickens. They had no need for pesos. He also brought a few packets of his favorite seed varieties, which he planned to offer in thanks for the feast that had just been served. As he opened up his bag, he pulled the Stockpile & Seed Catalog out of the way to get to the seeds.

The woman who had first shown him the chickens snatched it up and showed it to the others standing next to her. She opened it up and was mesmerized. The book was passed slowly across small groups of individuals, and their eyes widened as they turned page after page, not understanding the words, but comprehending each and every image devouring every last one as if it was the most delicious and holy meal.

Hector winked at George. "I think you have found something to barter with."

"What? The book?"

"No, senior, what you offer inside!" He explained to the villagers that any plant or seed that they saw in the catalog could be theirs in exchange for some chickens, and he reported back to George that they had a deal.

On Wednesday morning, they found a neat stack of numerous crates filled with roosters and hens and even baby chicks inside. They were piled up high next to their plane. There was also a young boy sitting waiting for them. "Yo voy," he said to George.

George looked at Hector and asked, "What is he saying?"

"I think he's saying he's planning to go with us."

George looked at the young man and tousled his hair. "We'd love to take you along little amigo, but just where do you think you're going?"

"Yo voy!" he said again firmly to George.

George looked at Hector and shrugged. Hector spoke to the boy and then turned to George. "He is insurance. They are sending him along with you to insure that you actually bring back the seeds you have promised."

To this end, the boy handed the catalog to George and showed where dozens of pages had been folded down and numerous pictures had been circled.

"Well, alrighty then. That's asombroso!"
They loaded up the plane and tied the
crates down to secure them. Hector got in
the rear pilot seat, and the boy and
George climbed in. A crowd of native
onlookers came to see them off and yelled
"Adios, amigos!" as they taxied down the
field and took off.

They landed back at the original Mexican
village close to nightfall, and unloaded the
chicken crates into the back of the pickup.

Danielle took one look at the stack of
crates and pondered about the back of the
pickup. "HOW do we get them across the
border?" Not only did they have a long
drive in front of them, suddenly it dawned
on everyone that they had completely
forgotten about customs and inspections.
The birds could be indefinitely detained.
They certainly would never survive any
kind of quarantine. Inoculations given in
the past had killed many a bird. There
had to be an alternative plan.

HEIRLOOM!

Danielle piped up, "We could put them in a giant piñata!"

Hector mumbled, "We could stuff the chicks into the wheels of your truck…" The horror of what they might endure made them all shudder.

George said, "I have a brainstorm! We could drive to a border area and throw them over the fence and then drive around and round them up later." But the vision of trying to chase and round up wild chickens in an unfenced countryside flashed across their collective brains and they all shook their heads.

Danielle spoke, "We could set them free by the fence and put some enticing chicken feed out on the other side to entice them to fly a central location."

George replied, "Chickens don't fly."

"Oh."

HEIRLOOM!

Then the words came out of Hector's mouth, "Fly. Si! Fly. I will fly them to your Faire!"

"That's asombroso!"

HEIRLOOM!

1 O.

One of the highlights of the lecture circuit part of the Faire, was the various 'celebrities.' There was Mason Green the Survival Chef who advocated eating weeds in the wild, Janice and Justin off-grid New York City homesteaders who showed how to make electricity from their rooftop potato patch, and Lakshmi Vishaal an international Indian activist for GMO-free agriculture who was the only International part of the show's lineup (putting the "inter" in the International Heirloom Faire name), who had a fanatical cult-like following. Another crowd favorite of many garden enthusiasts was William Stanton, of the "Slow Down Your Food" and the "Raise Your Own Rations" social media channels.

Willie, as his friends called him, began to document his life on camera over a dozen years ago. He started sharing his videos at pop-up health events and later online. After years of daily sharing, he had amassed close to four thousand videos! With the advent of live streaming, he was an ever-present fixture popping up randomly on many people's social streams. He also started a cookware website selling pots and pans, steamers, juicers, blenders, and just about everything, including kitchen sinks.

When doing official lectures, he often told his story of overcoming the odds and surviving a very serious near fatal hospital infection. Nearly fifteen years ago, he was told he was going to die. He turned his life over to God and a Garden of Eden diet. He subsisted on steamed vegetables and had a full miraculous reversal of his symptoms. He began to eat only healthy foods and eschewed all fast food and shared every step of the way. He'd say, "Slow down your food." and "Take time to stop and smell the spices."

His story was a moving one and heartfelt. It always evoked gasps of empathy from the audience, even those that had heard it before. Tears would well up in his eyes as he spoke about the moment when he thought he was going to die and how it all changed for him. The audience was always spellbound. They respected his vulnerable and sensitive nature. Only today, he was especially disconsolate.

He had a very public relationship with his vegan girlfriend, Cherise, who began showing up in his videos about a year or so back. A dark-haired beauty, she looked at him with glowing admiration onscreen and hovered by his side. But while Willie was at ease onscreen, when he asked

HEIRLOOM!

Cherise to speak into the camera she seemed uncomfortable.

What the audience did not know was that the previous night Cherise had left Willie.

Willie was dedicated to transforming the world one video at a time. He would seize any opportunity to tape any valuable lesson, no matter how small. On Tuesday, Willie caught wind of Compost Joe's recent legal altercation with the community and he decided to interview him about it. He let Cherise know he'd be about an hour and a half and that he'd meet her for a late dinner at the hotel. When Willie and Joe got to talking about compost and cows and raising rations, the time flew by. Joe offered to drive Willie to the factory to smell firsthand the alleged noxious odors to see if he was offended. Willie, of course, jumped at the chance and they headed to the countryside as the sky darkened. An hour and a half side trip turned into three. With no cell signal on the way, he assumed that Cherise would lovingly understand his tardiness since he had such a momentous opportunity to film and share this journey.

She did not.

She laid down the ultimatum: "Me or the video camera." The camera won and she left.

Then this morning, he saw Cherise in the food vendor area snuggled up next to and gazing admirably at Paleo Diet YouTuber, Mitch, the host of the "Grass Fed Meat Matters" channel, and eating barbeque pork ribs! Shocked and bewildered, he staggered away aghast that his "vegan" girlfriend would turn on a dime in such a manner.

Today in the Food and Family Hall, Willie regaled his tale of sitting outside the doctor's office being told he might die. He began to sob uncontrollably, all while streaming live to his fan base. Harold, who was there to keep an eye on Willie's camera, grew concerned. His eyes widened

HEIRLOOM!

as he had never seen Willie quite this emotional before. He'd seen him moody with a tear now and then, but not this manic.

Harold motioned to Willie motioning his hand across his throat to see if he wanted to stop rolling.

Willie waggled his head and said, "No man. I'm okay," temporarily pulling it together, only to burst out crying again.

He managed to finish the talk a little worse for the wear. Harold came up and gave him a big brother hug and offered him his flask. "You want a shot, bro?"

Willie politely declined, packed up his stuff and headed back to his hotel room.

Later that evening he checked his stats on that video of the day. It was going viral. He also saw a major bump in his sales performance on his cookware website. He nodded pleasantly to himself, smiled, curled up around a pillow, and fell asleep.

HEIRLOOM!

11.

On Thursday, in the late afternoon, Chucky had been assigned to manage the Seed Exchange. Last year, it had turned into the equivalent of a Wal-Mart Black Friday frenzy. He expected no less from this year's Faire.

While waiting for the usual antics to begin, one of the volunteers, JoJo, approached Chucky to report a lost squash stash. JoJo had been one of the squash picker volunteers. He had set aside a special selection of 'the best of the best' to present to the annual end-of-show squash stew. "I knew they would be good eating. I guess someone else knew it, too." But aside from this petty theft, the day was essentially calmer and less eventful than the two previous days. This he knew, however, would be changing come three o'clock.

The morning milking demonstrations had gone off without a hitch and been a success with none of the usual skirmishes. Every day around lunch, he had to cruise by the baby animal display. He'd stand there admiring the sweet little piglets while chomping on a honey-cured ham and organic Swiss sandwich on gluten-free multigrain, (never making the connection between piglets and the sandwich he munched on). He adored their twisty little tails on their round rumps, their milky pink short silky hair, and their sweet little upturned snouts. He found those babies so much easier to take in than the school children who would show up for morning field trips and run around the grounds like wild animals, or worse, the infantile 'savages' who showed up at the seed swap.

After the piglets, he headed back towards the Vendor Hall. The smell of a skunk wafted through the fairgrounds. It was like a cross between bitter coffee brewing and tar. He worried he might be called on to investigate it. But then, he thought ironically that that might be a better fate for him than the annual seed swap antics.

Chucky then proceeded to head to the north end of the Exhibit Hall where watermelon tasting was going on, and saw three long folding tables had been setup. Ten minutes to go. No one arrived yet. It always started out so innocently.

The first to arrive were two Asian women, empty handed. "Is this where the free seeds are?"

"This is a seed EXCHANGE, ladies. It is for people with seeds to trade then with other people who have seeds to offer."

HEIRLOOM!

They nodded in acknowledgement and stuck around anyways.

Then a few more straggled by: a mixed couple, a Middle Eastern man in a keffiyeh and his white wife dressed all in white linen with a stuffed wrinkled brown paper lunch bag in hand. Another middle-aged Caucasian urban-looking well-dressed couple that looked like they had just left a Sonoma County wine tasting wandered in. An older hippie dude with long grey hair in a ponytail put down a box of plastic baggies and a black marker on the table. Many variations of the young, wannabe-a-weed-farmer-looking guys were always present. A young women with an unknown South American accent said she had seeds and wanted to know who else had them. The conversations began. And, as more and more people arrived, it got harder and harder to differentiate between all the personalities.

HEIRLOOM!

The first seed packets got strewn all over the first table, and the entire mass of people lunged towards that table. Hands went grabbing for whatever they could clasp. The blending of voices began. "What is that?" "How do you germinate it?" "Who has hemp seeds?" "I dunno what they are. They're not labeled." "Hey, I was going to grab that one." "Where are you growing those?" "That is my stack." "Thank you so much." "Wanna share those?" "Give that back to me." "I'm bringing them back to Canada, eh." "Please stop shoving." "Are those organic or regular?" "You'll get yours. Be patient." "Who just elbowed me?" "Where does that grow?"

For the first ten minutes or so, overall, it seemed to be running fairly smoothly. Over time, even more people showed up with more seeds and more grasping hands while others took their early booty and left. A thirty year-old African American woman arrived with a stack of several round plastic containers. She set them on the third table and started to methodically spoon out little piles of seeds into small manila coin envelopes. "Make sure you label each seed. And, make sure you put my name, Shirley Ross, on each one so you'll remember I'm the one that gave them to you. My email is also here so please send me pictures of what you are able to grow. I love getting pictures." Then he heard it. Two of the pot-head planters were in each other's faces over at table number two.

"What's your problem man? There's enough seed for everyone."

"I was just trying to get that bag of Moringa. It was the last one."

"Well, if you were a gentleman you would not be pushing the little ladies aside to get it."

"There you've done it. Now it's gone. Someone else grabbed it."

"Someone must have needed it more than you, dude."

HEIRLOOM!

"F*#! you man. You don't know me or what I need."

The crowd started to give them just a little space without leaving the tables and losing their chance to pick up more precious seeds.

"Woah, dude. Chill."

"No you chill. I needed that Moringa seed."

"Dude, they're selling little plants over in the Vending Hall."

"I want to grow my own from scratch."

A man a few feet away chimed in. "I have some seeds I'll share with you."

"That's not the point. This jerk pushed me aside."

"Yah, well you pushed her out of the way first, dude," he said, pointing to a young adjacent lady. "Like this," and the example push was given from one dude to another. And in the next instant, the fisticuffs began.

HEIRLOOM!

Chucky leapt into the middle of it and grabbed one of the guys by the collar as the other took a tumble and hit his hip on the table, knocking half the share inventory off it. In a rush, people scrambled to pick them up.

"Break it up. Break it up. No seeds for you! Next! Nobody fights at my fair!" And Chucky snapped his fingers.

"But man, this f*#!-wad started it."

"You're pushing your luck little man. You're banished from all future seed exchanges. Now go and cool off some place. And watch your language. This is a family event. There are children around." Thinking to himself... and you two are the most childish of them all.

To the first guy, he said, "You. Go around to the left of the barn hall and visit the little baby piggies." And to the other, "You. Go around to the right of the barn hall and visit the little baby calves. See if you can appreciate the finer things in life beside seeds."

Both guys shook themselves off and headed their separate ways.

After the scuffle, the crowd became more subdued and polite. One strikingly tall gentleman seed bearer stood away from the tables with his offerings and calmly bartered with individuals one-on-one. He was the last one to finally depart at about an hour after the swapping began.

Chucky counted himself lucky that no third parties were injured in the encounter. He breathed a sigh of relief as he opened the storage closet with one of his many keys, so the volunteers could put away folding tables. The altercation had been a minimal exchange. Chucky headed back out into the sunlight and held his hand up towards the bright disc heading on its final descent towards the horizon. It was the last afternoon of a memorable few days. He was going to miss the excitement once he got back to the docks. Since his walkie-talkie radio was silent and there were no further pressing demands for the day, he decided to head back to the baby farm animals.

There they were, "Mr. and Mr. Seed," chatting agreeably by the chickens. "A couple of dicks by the cocks," he thought. They were leaning on the fence, each with one foot up on the first rung turned towards each other. He thought, "Well, that's nice, they worked it out. There's nothing like the baby animals to bring out the best nature in everybody. Kind of makes you want to have some little baby critters of your own."

And then he thought about one of the cute girls handing out drinks over at the kombucha stand, and figured he'd head over there to get her number. He began to turn and head towards the Food Hall, but did a double take when he saw the potty mouth guy reach for, and rest his hand tenderly on, the other guy's hand.

HEIRLOOM!

"Well, Jiminy Cricket. I should have sent them to the Dahlia Displays."

1 2.

By the time Thursday had rolled around, Harold had not slept more than a few hours over the course of three days. This combined with his penchant for all of the fine fermented beverages sampled at the fairgrounds and in the surrounding countryside, he was fairly tipsy by noon everyday and well lubricated by the afternoon. How he made it through each night was nothing short of an astonishing phenomenon. He was spurred along by the late-into-the-evening, after-show festivities and gatherings with flute and drum jams. A cloud of sweet herbal smoke would linger around these impromptu get-togethers.

The leader of these jams was Harold's long-time festival buddy, Kurt. Kurt was an erudite and undersized man of many talents, one of them being Native American flute playing. He was also a virtuoso traditional flautist, but his talent was always upstaged by his form of dress. He wore plaid tights and a puffy shirt and red crocs. He became known in the inner circle as the Pied Piper of Crimson Creek, although most people called him the Petite Pied Piper or 'PPP,' but never directly to his face. In any case, whenever he held these late night jams, the pretty ladies always seemed to follow.

The young college girl volunteers would show up dancing in their cotton gauze skirts and skimpy t-shirts with bright colored wooden beads and crystals circling their necks. Harold especially appreciated the just-out-of-sight 'Namaste' cleavage tattoo on one particular dancer. These apparitions kept him up at night. And he was awoken a few scant hours later with some last minute adjustments to sound and video systems, or some speaker who lost his box of books. Another speaker lost his entire presentation on 'Breeding Goats for Milk Production' when his thumb drive was freakishly dropped in a vat of sauerkraut. Some believed this was more than mere coincidence, as a rival speaker was giving a presentation on a related 'Sheep Cheese - Not Baaahd' topic in another hall.

In any case, it was finally here, the closing talk of the show was taking place in the Farm and Garden Hall. Harold was to interview his dear old friend, Scotty, on growing organic corn. Scotty was a soft spoken man with fond philosophical feelings for tender corn. He also was prone to go off on interesting, but long-winded, tangents. Scotty was a very pure spirit who spent day and night surrounded by his beloved plants. He was also one of those people who was very enthusiastic about telling a story, without regard to whether or not the listener cared to here it, beginning to end. One got the sense that he must have talked for hours on end to his plants while alone, and they patiently endured and soaked up his loving words. Yet he seemed to forget that people had more limited attention spans.

Scotty started his presentation announcing that he would begin with a poem to the 'Great Corn.'

"Dear Great Corn.

"I'm looking forward to your arrival on Harvest Night.

"I hope you will bring me lots of kernels to eat."

Scotty's voice was so low, that the microphone was not picking it up. So Harold pushed the mic closer to him.

"Dear Great Corn.

"I'm looking forward to your arrival on Harvest Night…"

Scotty sat up straighter, putting his voice box further away from the mic. Harold moved the mic closer. Scotty backed away even more, as if the metallic foreign object would bite him.

"Dear Great Corn…"

Harold reached over and nudged Scotty on the back to get him closer to the mic and whispered, "Think of it as an ear of corn." It seemed to work, as Scotty settled in and restarted the poem a fourth time in a mellifluous voice.

"Dear Great Corn.

"I'm looking forward to your arrival on Harvest Night.

"I hope you will bring me lots of kernels to eat.

"During harvest, the Great Corn spike tassels rise in height,

"High on the stalk, silks brown and Great Corn grows sweet.

HEIRLOOM!

"The wind flies the pollen through the air for the good little ears.

"Sit with me in the corn patch to watch the hairy tufts of silk.

"While we look forward to golden, big, juicy spears,

"And scrape off every precious drop of delicious corn milk.

"The tomato may be number one and most loved of all.

"Let's face it, it has more publicity; gets more media hype.

"Being number two, Great Corn must try harder each fall.

"It takes a full twenty days to get fully ripe!"

Harold's eyes drooped and shut. The sound of a snoring snort came over the speakers as his head nodded down. Shawn, the audio visual guy on the side, tried to throw a walnut at his head to wake him up and missed. The nut landed on the dais in front of him. A second one also landed on the table. Shawn threw another and caught Harold on the right shoulder, and he jerked up with a start, while Scotty continued his recitation

"Do not be a blockhead. Be not naive.

"Be ready for the Great Corn treats to appear.

"Do not be discouraged because of what you believe.

"He brings treats to the good children only once in a year."

Scotty glanced over at Harold, smiled serenely, and waxed on in his melodious tone:

"Say, I got a pumpkin. I got a pepper. I got a pear.

"But an ear of corn... that is my preferred preference.

"All are wonderful to eat, and of course, to share.

"We need not be separated by denominational difference."

Harold had nodded off again.

HEIRLOOM!

"Oh, Great Corn, where are you? It won't be long now.

"I will find a corn patch that is truly sincere.

"And I'll put in a good word for YOU when we go to plough.

"Oh, Great Corn, I'll be waiting. Same time next year."

Scotty ended his poem. There was a pregnant pause and polite applause. It was time for the interview to start, but Harold was completely down for the count. This time Shawn threw a walnut and it hit Scotty smack in the forehead. Without missing a beat. Scotty jumped up, and threw him arms up high and proclaimed. "The world's gone nuts!" Then he juggled the three nuts sitting on the platform. The crowd roared and Harold awoke.

Shawn got up on stage and conducted the interview, while Harold wandered off back stage and no one saw him again until much later that night.

HEIRLOOM!

13.

The Faire always ran from Tuesday to
Thursday. This was to appease the
Saturday Sabbath regulations of the
various religious factions involved in the
event production. Also, as a seed
company, a weekday event was in line
with the normal work schedule. This
meant the weekend afterwards would be
open for rest and frivolity. This never
seemed to happen though, as the event
wrap-up always took more than a few
days to complete.

HEIRLOOM!

But for the record, Thursday was closing night. The vendors were contracted to stay open until eight PM, but most began to pack up their wares in the Vendor Hall by six, so they could either escape the grounds or join the closing ceremonies when the staff and the volunteers gathered in the main display hall to eat all the displayed vegetables. In the final remaining hours of the Faire, a crew of volunteers cleaned and cut up all the squash and vegetables they could gather. These were thrown into the biggest soup pot you ever did see which was cooked down for an hour or more for the best tasting stew ever.

Thursday morning started in a panic for Christine. Her box of honey sticks was gone! Immediately assuming the worst (and after a near meltdown), Christine went into her can-do attitude and headed directly to the dumpster in back and found herself digging through rotting orange rinds and organic coffee grounds. When the office volunteers came out to get her, they found her two feet waving in the air and pulled her out.

They let her know that someone had tidied the office and moved her honey stick supply. They were uncovered under a box of hazelnut butter samples. Breathing a huge sigh of relief and dusting herself off, Christine proceeded to make the final rounds of the various halls and exhibits to make sure everything was winding down peacefully. It was a sad moment. She looked at the pot of stew in the making, and she got misty thinking that this was the first year ever that George had not been present for the show. His show. Most people were aware that George was not there. But they were so busy with their various duties and responsibilities, that they didn't have time to miss him. Now that things were wrapping up, however, there was a feeling of melancholy throughout the halls, with the realization that their intrepid leader had not been there to witness their earnest work and say his usual, "That's amazing!"

She must have been psychic, because at that very moment her walkie-talkie crackled with news. She had left her cell phone in the office sometime back and apparently it had been ringing off the hook. Danielle was trying to call her. She finally got in touch with another Crimson Creek employee. Danielle wanted Christine to know that George was on his way post haste. He needed an all-clear to get permission to do an emergency landing on the infield of the fairground racing track. SOS. Could she help?

Christine perked up. She broke out a celebration honey stick!!! The activity in the hall took on a whole new characteristic to her. Kurt and his flutist tune seemed somehow brighter. The stew smelled more delicious. She looked over at Chucky. He smiled and gave her a smile and a, "How's it going?" look with a thumbs up. She waved to him excitedly to come over. She told him about the news that George would be arriving by plane any moment now and they had to make sure safety and security was being taken care of. They had to get a crew out to the racetrack and make sure the center turf was clear and safe.

The stew would have to wait.

Compost Joe found out next and high-fived Scotty. Scotty let out a whoop and began to juggle some jujubes. As news spread throughout the hall, more people piled out filling the racetrack grandstands to witness George's impending dramatic arrival. Petite Pied Piper led the way.

14.

Thursday morning, they were packed up again, fully fueled, and ready to go.

"Yo voy," the Mexican boy said to George.

They had all forgotten about the young man.

Feeling a déjà vous. George looked at the young man and tousled his hair again. "We'd love to take you along little amigo, but there will not be enough room for you and the chickens and Dan."

"Yo voy!" he said emphatically again to George.

Danielle then quietly spoke up, "If it's alright with you boss, I'd like to stay here a while."

George looked at Danielle with understanding and affection, and then looked at the Shaman standing next to her.

"Take good care of her Shaman. She's a rare and precious gem." And as an afterthought added, "She's a genuine first class car on the Orient Express!"

The Shaman smiled and shook his head up and down.

Then to the little boy, "All righty then. You voy!"

To Hector he said, "Let's get your bird, and my birds, off the ground. We have uno Faire to catch!"

Hector calculated, "By my calculations it will be close, but that fairground racetrack infield that you spoke of should be just long enough for us to land."

"Dan please find a phone, any phone, and call ahead to Christine. Let her know we're on our way. We should get there before dark. We need to make sure that turf is clear and ready for landing." He gave her a final hug and popped into the plane.

The three amigos sped off into the big blue sky, Hector in back and George and the boy holding down the front pit with crates of chickens strapped in. By the time they got close to the fairgrounds, George had allowed himself a little shuteye. The drone of the engines and wind in his hair made him sleepy. It had been a harrowing adventure, a bit more stressful than he had expected, but all was well that was ending well.

He woke when his stomach felt the bottom fall out. The plane was making its final descent towards the racetrack. Hector had circled around once to get a good look at his landing location, and was doing a last double check approach over the racetrack. The sun was just setting and the glow over the grandstand filling up with people was spectacular.

George was so busy admiring the colorful Faire grounds, picking out and identifying each hall, and enjoying the bird's eye view of the show he had created. He did not immediately notice that the young boy had opened up each and every crate. He said in his unique dialect of Spanish, "Why don't you let the birds arrive in style and fly down?"

George yelled back to Hector, "What did he just say?" Hector shouted, "I think he said, 'Why don't you let the birds arrive in style and fly?'"

George screamed, but it was too late, "Chickens can't fly!" The birds fluttered outside the boxes and the wind whipped up their wings and out they all went for better or for worse.

HEIRLOOM!

The origins of common chickens are jungle fowl. These ancient ancestors from India and Asia could fly only short distances to roost in trees and escape predators. Their body mass was too large to support real flight. So flying any great distances, even those ancestral wild birds, they could not.

The vision of dozens of chickens pouring down on the Faire guests splattering the sidewalk with a blood sacrifice flashed across George's imagination. In that moment, he saw the end of his beloved festival... The next day's news would be.

"Things really 'fowled' up at the I.H.F.!"

"Faire organizer 'pullets' a fast one, and a brutal publicity stunt goes awry!"

"Heirloom Faire is all fried up... with plummeting poultry!"

"Annual Fall Festival Bombs... Chickens!"

HEIRLOOM!

"Oh, the humanity!" He thought. George restrained himself from wringing the boy's neck, closed his eyes and prayed and prayed and prayed.

Hector lined himself up with the grandstand and used his peripheral vision to assess his height and tracking and brought the plane down for a challenging, but successful landing.

The crowd was roaring. George opens his eyes, hearing the screaming at the devastation and looked around for the massacre, but did not see any. The crowd was not screaming in anger. It was cheering. There were live chickens out on the field with a few more coming in for landing behind them.

It was an heirloom miracle!

This rare heritage breed had developed an unusual capacity for flight never known to any common domestic, or even any previously known, breeds. Due to a freak adaptation to their jungle environment, it was a long way down, but their expanded and untrimmed wing capacity helped them manage to float and flap their way down to the fairgrounds as the plane set down on the field. They were already busy clucking and pecking on the field. They had worked up an appetite.

As George stepped out of the cockpit in shock and wonder, Christine and Chucky were running towards him to embrace him. A larger crowd caught up with them cheering and gathered around George to lift him on their shoulders and carry him back to the Exhibit Hall to celebrate with stew! Hector was welcomed and congratulated by those remaining. No one seemed to notice the young Mexican Boy whistling and making calls to the hens and roosters, rounding them up and herding them back to their crates, as they obediently complied.

15.

It was close to eleven PM. Most everyone had gone home or back to their campsites and hotel rooms. George, Hector and Christine sat on benches around a fire ring in the fairground picnic area near the bandstand. The Mexican boy crouched at the fireside, poking it with a stick.

Chucky strolled up and announced that he had done his last rounds and all was quiet on the Faire front. He sat down and joined them. "That was quite a stunt you pulled off today. My only advice is to get rid of

HEIRLOOM!

the evidence before the authorities start asking questions tomorrow." He nodded to the boy.

George looked over at the kid and then at Hector who said, "I cannot fly my plane por la noche, senior."

"He'll be okay, Chucky. We are taking care of him."

Out of nowhere, Harold stumbled into view, a bit disheveled and quite woozy. "Am I imagining things or is there a beautiful vintage by-plane out on the field? Oh, hi George. Where's Danielle?"

"She's in Mexico."

"Oh. Who's this?" pointing at the boy.

"I dunno. What is your name son?"

The kid looked up, knowing he was being addressed but did not answer."

"Como te llamas?" asked Hector.

HEIRLOOM!

Proudly spoken, "Mi llama es Miguel Don Juan de Sanchez Alexander Borrego." He added an affirmative nod at the end.

Harold woozily said, "Quite a big name for a little guy."

"Tomorrow are taking Miguel over to the Stockpile and putting a care package together for him to take back to his village in gratitude for their gifts," George explained.

"Oh, yes. The chickens... That explains the plane. Someone told me about that. It's a blessed bantam miracle!"

There was a collective sigh.

Christine spoke to Harold, "You know the Bearded Booch 'n' Brew Boys donated a couple of leftover promotional cases of their wares. They're in the office. You are welcome to use them as you wish."

Harold let out a hoot, and sobered right up. "Jumpin' JehhhhHoooVah!" He pulled out his cell phone and speed dialed Kurt. "Bring on the dancing girls. We got ourselves a party... Yes... Couple of cases... Bearded Brew... In about ten... Okay, I'll grab a cart.... See ya."

While this conversation was going on, Christine looked at George. "So Danielle is where?"

Hector jumped in, "She is en las manos buenas... the best of hands. Our Shaman is sincere. And I have never seen him spontaneously outburst like that. They must be 'amantes.'" He said it wistfully and romantically, "Past life lovers."

Christine's eyebrows raised up.

"And speaking of past lives. It is past my bedtime. I will take Miguel back to my room. Gracias to you for arranging a room, Miss Christina. Jorge is very lucky to have such an associate, simpatico and inteligente." And he kissed her hand.

"Buenos noches amigos! Hasta mañana."

"Hasta mañana," said all three in unison.

HEIRLOOM!

Christine looked longingly after Hector and the boy. "I must learn to speak Spanish."

Chucky added, "Interesting about Danielle. Love must be in the air. I think I'll go investigate Harold's dancing girls. Well, good night folks."

The fire was dwindling and it was just Christine and George left peacefully staring at the coals. Christine handed George a honey stick and together they sucked on them thoughtfully until the fire died out. George got up, dowsed the embers, and held his hand out to Christine to help her out of her seat.

"Well, I'd best be getting home to the little women. Christine, you have been more than amazing. You have been... Asombroso!" By this point, he had become very proud of his bilingual abilities.

As they headed towards the parking lot, Christine spoke up, "George..."

"Yes, Christine."

HEIRLOOM!

"Next time you decide to take off on a wild goose chase, please don't do it during Faire week. Be a good egg, and please fly South in the winter."

ABOUT THE AUTHOR

Mary-Margaret (anand sahaja) Stratton is a Renaissance woman whose expertise spans a number of subjects: published poet, accomplished musical composer, prolific author, lay architect, instruction designer, painter, sculptor, festival producer, educator, and Award-Winning Creative Art Director. She has degrees in Marketing, and Design from UCLA. In 2011, anand was ordained as an Essene Minister. Anand was born and raised in the City of Angels and is currently on the Advisory Board for *Valley Relics Museum*.

HEIRLOOM!

She has been married for over twenty five years. She and her husband write music, make movies, dance, travel, teach raw chocolate classes, plant gardens, and have been dedicated Historic Preservationists who restored multiple Modern homes, and were recipients of the Las Vegas *MUDA, Mayor's Urban Design Award.* When not pursuing other eclectic endeavors, she likes to watch movies with happy endings.

HEIRLOOM!

ADDITIONAL BOOKS BY THE AUTHOR:

Dominant Health (Contributing Editor) (rawmatt.com)

Eat Like Eve (Contributing Author) (eatlikeeve.com)

Good Wiccan Guides (goodwiccan.com)

How Modern Was My Valley (howmodernwasmyvalley.com)

Kiss Addiction Goodbye (12stepdiet.com)

Living in Sin ~ Mondo Las Vegas (futurahouse.com)

Marry and Grow Happy (with Mr. Stratton) (marryandgrow.com)

Please Don't Eat My Friends (Contributing Author) (cherrycapri.com)

Pop Tags (futurahouse.com)

Stop Picking on Me & SPOM! Workbook (stoppickingonme.com)

HEIRLOOM!

HEIRLOOM!

EPILOGUE

The moon had set and it was about an hour to dawn. Pied Piper Kurt was passed out on a picnic bench with empty Booch 'n' Brews strewn about. Harold and Chucky were deeply engrossed in trying to names strains of weed in alphabetical order. Afghan Kush, Bob Saget, Cat Piss, Dopium, East Coast Alien, Fat Albert… but when they got to Golden Goat, they forgot what letter they were on and had to start over again.

A lone girl was left playing a melancholy tune on autoharp. Harold nodded to Chucky and said, "I think she's been waiting for you."

Chucky rolled his eyes and said, "Not my type."

To which Harold replied, "I admit, she's a little odd. But look at that long angelic hair."

HEIRLOOM!

Chucky sized her up again more closely and a bit bleary-eyed.

Slowly Garth looked up from the harp and directly at Chucky and gave him a sly wink.

www.ingramcontent.com/pod-product-compliance
Lightning Source LLC
Chambersburg PA
CBHW052007220626
47052CB00004B/1134